SHREK 2™
THE POTION PLAN

Adapted by Gail Herman

Pencils by Isidre Mones

Color by SI International

Scholastic Reader — Level 3

SCHOLASTIC INC.

New York Toronto London Auckland Sydney
Mexico City New Delhi Hong Kong Buenos Aires

ISBN: 0-439-63401-6

Shrek is a registered trademark of DreamWorks L.L.C. Shrek 2, Shrek Ears and Shrek "S" design ™ and © 2004 DreamWorks L.L.C.

Published by Scholastic Inc.
SCHOLASTIC, CARTWHEEL BOOKS, and associated logos are trademarks and/or registered trademarks of Scholastic Inc.

12 11 10 9 8 7 6 5   4 5 6 7 8/0

Printed in the U.S.A.
First printing, May 2004

Shrek and Princess Fiona
had just married.

Now, Shrek was meeting Fiona's parents,
the King and Queen of Far Far Away.

The King looked at Shrek.
He was shocked.
This was Fiona's husband? An ogre?
What about Prince Charming?
The one Fiona was supposed to marry?
Of course, Fiona was an ogre, too.

But the King knew that could change.
One spell from her Fairy Godmother
and — presto!
Fiona would be beautiful.
But a beautiful princess married to an ogre?
Never!

Shrek thought Fiona agreed with the King.
She really does want a Prince Charming,
he decided.
So he and Donkey and their new friend
Puss In Boots went to see the Fairy
Godmother.

"I don't want to be an ogre,"
Shrek told the Fairy Godmother.
"I want to be a handsome prince."

But the Fairy Godmother had her
own ideas.
She wanted Shrek out of her factory.
And out of Fiona's life.

"You want to do Fiona a favor?"
the Fairy Godmother asked.
"Go back to your swamp, ogre!"

But Shrek would not go.
"We have to get what we came for," he said.
The Fairy Godmother wouldn't help him.
Maybe he could help himself.
But how? Shrek wondered.
A magic potion! That's what he needed.

On the factory floor, he saw a boiling
cauldron. Elves bustled about.
And animals in cages quacked,
hooted, and squeaked.

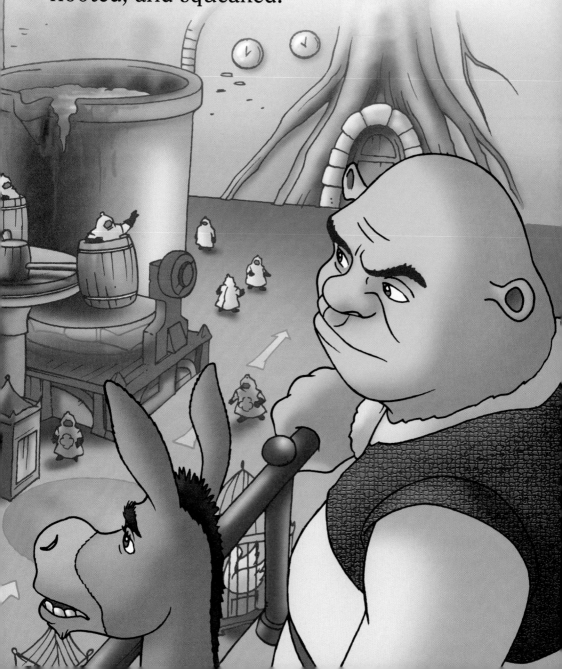

Then Shrek saw a door.
Its sign read: Potion Room.
Quickly, Shrek put on a factory uniform.
He waved Donkey and Puss into a cart.
Then, he pushed them right past the guards.
They were inside the Potion Room!

Inside, Shrek saw hundreds of bottles.
All he needed was *one*.
One potion to make him a handsome
prince.

"Puss," said Shrek.
"Climb up the shelves.
Read the potion labels.
Look under H for handsome."

Puss climbed.
"I can't find Handsome," he reported.
"But there is a Happily Ever After.
And it says something about beauty!"

Puss yanked the bottle.
Potions tumbled to the floor.
Glass smashed.
Alarms rang.
Surprised, Puss dropped the potion.

Donkey dove — and caught the bottle!
But then, he swallowed it!
Shrek couldn't do anything.
Guards were running toward them.
"Run!" he cried to Donkey and Puss.

But already guard elves were closing in.
Shrek flung Puss over one shoulder.
He tucked Donkey under the other arm.

"What are you doing?" shouted Donkey.
Shrek didn't answer.
He tipped over the boiling cauldron.

Potion spilled across the floor.
It swept over everything.
Elves ran everywhere.
Shrek grabbed a giant hook.
He swung over the floor . . .
And landed — thud!
The bottle flew out of Donkey's mouth.

Shrek and his friends ran into the forest.
They stopped to rest.
Shrek looked at the bottle of magic potion.
Would it help?
Donkey drank some.
Nothing happened.

Shrek drank some.
Nothing happened.
Maybe it didn't work on donkeys
and ogres.

When Shrek and Donkey woke up the next morning, they were different. "I'm handsome!" Shrek cried.

"Look at me!" Donkey said. "I'm trotting! I can whinny! I'm gorgeous! I'm a noble steed!"

Shrek, Donkey, and Puss went
back to the castle.
Shrek thought that Fiona would be very
happy when she saw him.

Fiona had changed too.
She was a beautiful princess.
Shrek was a handsome prince.
But the potion would wear off.

There was only one way to stay beautiful.
"Kiss me," Shrek told Fiona,
"before the clock strikes midnight,
and we can stay this way forever!"

"But I was happy before," Fiona said.
"I want the old Shrek back."

They didn't kiss.
And they didn't stay beautiful.
They became ogres again.
Donkey became Donkey again.
But that's exactly what they wanted.
Donkey grinned at Shrek and Fiona.
"Now I'd say that is happily ever after!"